S. L. SKINNER

100
HAIKUS
ABOUT
HORROR
MOVIES

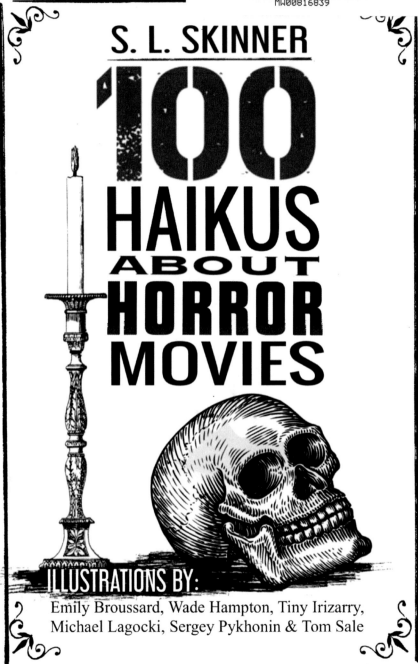

ILLUSTRATIONS BY:

Emily Broussard, Wade Hampton, Tiny Irizarry,
Michael Lagocki, Sergey Pykhonin & Tom Sale

edited by: Suza Kanon and Lori Polemenakos

cover design by Heather Blaikie

original illustrations by:

Emily Broussard, Wade Hampton, Tiny Irizarry,

Michael Lagocki, Sergey Pykhonin, and Tom Sale.

Copyright © 2024 S.L. Kanon

Diversified Media Press, Dallas TX

ISBN: 979-8-218-48358-6

Can you name the films in these haikus?

1)
Shark attacks the beach,
Men gather to attack beast.
Shark bites, blood flows red.

2)
Thief hides in motel.
He peeps. She showers. They stab.
Sister seeks. Finds mom.

3)
Evil child wears mask.
Grows up and escapes to slash.
Babysitter survives.

4)
Trapped in theater.
Bloodthirsty demons infect.
Giallo new wave.

5)
Voyeur Tom sees her.
Photographer hides his blade.
Strikes pose D.O.A.

6)
Raven-haired witch laughs.
Inquisitor hammers,
Nails on her death mask.

7)
Mutant snowman stabs.
FX cheese. Scary bath scene.
Death by antifreeze.

8)
Creature swims, breathes with gills.
Voyeur watching beauty swims by,
Underwater love.

9)
Bathing beauty suns,
Goes for swim in dark lagoon.
Menace nibbles toes.

10)
Head covered with sack.
Break Halloween rules and die.
Jack o' Lantern gore.

(11)
Who can survive night?
Haunted house & Vincent Price,
Winner-take-all frights.

Illustration by Tom Sale

12)
Summer camp flirtation.
Jason drowns, mom returns mad.
Counselors get slashed.

13)
Hockey mask from camp.
Horny teens meet gruesome end.
The virgin survives.

14)
Teen band slays old song.
Black metal hymn. Demon king.
Zombie murderfest.

15)
Knife gloved killer creep.
Sneaks into dreams to slash teens.
Nancy cannot sleep.

16)
Summer camp bullies die.
Mean Judy's curling iron is fried,
Angela's surprise.

17)
Camping in RV.
Creepy family attacks scene.
Fight back or meet death.

18)
Temple House lady,
snake seduces wearing boots.
Virgin sacrifice.

19)
Stay on the path, boys!
Drunk, lost in moors, werewolves bite.
Grows fur and sharp teeth.

20)
Full moon gypsy curse.
Guilt, hunger, longing to bite,
Werewolf breaks old chains.

21)
Cursed tomb in Egypt.
Robbers fall into traps, cold.
Death comes in mummy's chokehold.

22)
Worried for sick kid.
Demon possessed green vomit.
Head spins, priest falls dead.

23)
Antarctica cold.
Shapeshifter absorbs their flesh.
No escape, burn it.

24)
Cabin in the woods.
Evil awakes to kill all.
Necronomicon.

25)
Girlfriend now possessed.
Replaced his hand with chainsaw.
Hag locked in basement.

26)
Sober Jack gets job.
Bat swings, ax swings, all work, no play.
Haunted hotel shines.

Illustration by Wade Hamptom

27)
Puzzlebox opens door.
Pierced demons bring much pain.
Such sights to show you.

28)
Weaponized masks.
Hypnotized kids murder.
Hero battles lab.

29)
Gang killed Sugar's man.
Baron Samedi raises dead.
Shining zombie eyes.

30)
Mad scientist lab.
X-ray eye-drops boost his sight.
Sideshow act, too real.

31)
Spaceship distress call.
Evil in collapsed black hole,
Come hither fly trap.

32)
People-skin face mask.
Cannibal family dines in.
Chainsaw dance at dawn.

33)
Comet zombies kill.
Girls shoot up mall, found by lab.
Science favors few.

34)
Pool dig, Indian graves.
Don't go into the light, girl.
Evil tv buzz.

35)
Lycanthrope cop drinks,
Drives, murders bad guys. Cult rite,
Liquor & donuts.

36)
Christopher Lee vamp
Bites into your neck, then snap!
...Bride of Dracula.

37)
Inherits aunt's house,
Conjures sexy casserole.
Mistress of the dark.

38)
Ghost ship rolls in gloom,
Midnight leper revenants.
Hook-hand pirates slash.

39)
Scary clown under
Ground, "Everything floats down here."
Murders kids with fear.

40)
Vampire Bowie ages.
Science meets "forever" love.
Drinks blood. Sexy kills.

41)
Armless knife thrower.
Hidden serial killer.
Circus girl recoils.

42)
Government issue
Ghouls in drums. Leaked zombie gas.
Dances nude on graves.

Illustration by Michael Lagocki

43)
Trapeze artist trick.
Gooble Gobble, One of Us
Creeps underneath

44)
Ripley and the cat.
Wake up to find Invaders.
Battles queen till death.

45)
Mean girls at school.
Telepath kills with bug swarm. Bullies are no more.

46)
Alien clowns
Murder a small town. Popcorn eats,
Cotton candy sucks.

47)
Angela invites
Teens to haunted house party.
Demon dance slasher.

48)
Art meets haunted house.
Sandworms. *Handbook of the Dead.*
Bio-exorcist.

49)
Mad scientist tests
Transporter on self. Sticky
Insect transformed zap.

50)
Boomstick time travel.
Ash battles skeleton foes,
Forgot magic words.

51)
Shaky cam jump scare.
Forest witch spooks. Crew now gone.
Haunted found footage.

52)
Cop seeks missing girl.
Island pagans draw him in,
Effigy cage fire.

53)
"See me," he whispers.
His mind calls her to his bite.
She dies, willingly.

54)
Ginger kids' cult farm.
Scarecrow in cornfield bleeds red,
Adults sacrificed.

55)
Copycat in mask
Kills all her friends till at last,
Final girl sequels.

56)
Barb runs from zombies.
Ben defends house, Harry
hides out from escape.

57)
Lands copter on mall.
Zombies shop till they drop shot.
Human plague lingers.

58)
Rescued from zombies.
Soldiers tease dead, then steal girls.
Re-populate fail.

59)
Tooth fairy leaves bites.
Doc Lector cooks and profiles
Prison pen pal kills.

60)
Lodge in dark forest
Secret lair for mad science,
Frees creature features.

61)
Alaskan darkness.
Rage vampire holiday month
Bites and hunts with traps.

62)
Cursed black prince,
Blood drinking thirst persists. Bites
Hot girls, mesmerized.

63)
Sunglasses can see:
"Consume, sleep, obey, conform;"
Hidden aliens.

64)
Kids wake up witches.
Halloween candle magic
Must defeat by dawn.

65)
Revenant artist.
Kills with hook and bees.
Says name in mirror.

66)
Doc mows down love
Builds new girl with hooker parts.
So high they explode.

67)
Silver ball of death.
Mausoleum as portal.
Other world. Hooded fiends.

68)
Teens go walk about,
Find dark compound in outback.
Torture ends in death.

69)
Dark. Girls' boarding school.
Giallo ballet of blood.
Dance coven murders.

70)
Young wife is with child.
Creepy factor set to high.
Satanic, they smile.

71)
Bad boys look for fun,
Find brothel of vampire girls.
Kills with broken heart.

72)
Antichrist kid kills.
"Did it for you, Damien."
Birthmark of the beast.

73)
Mop boy chased falls in.
Toxic waste he must avenge.
Defends citizens.

74)
Alien slugs raise the dead.
Ax murderer haunts cop.
Sorority flamethrower.

75)
Her feline ways cursed.
Love unconsummated. Lust
Smolders, transforms, kills.

76)
Semi-trucks circle.
Victims huddle in diner.
Hit and run gremlin.

77)
Beatnik gallery.
Successful sculptures make
Murder into art.

78)
Victor builds a man
Of corpse parts with new brain pan,
Angry mob. Fire bad.

79)
Doctor builds a wife.
Corpse parts & big hair fright.
Rejects his monster.

Illustration by Michael Lagocki

80)
Atomic kaiju.
Flying lizard stomps, smashes,
wrecks Tokyo, breathes fire.

81)
Doc West looks for parts.
Re-animate for science,
Angry killer corpses.

82)
Basque blacksmith hermit's
Boobytraps capture demons:
Devil in the flesh.

83)
Orphan in Spain's war
sees ghosts. Blood floats up.
Bullies kill, seek gold.

84)
Girl marries man with sis.
Bloody ghosts. Gothic mansion.
Black widower kills.

85)
Ginger teen bullied
By mean girls and mom's god till
Psychic triggered, kills.

Illustration by Emily Broussard

86)
Wicked carnival
Parades through town, promises
Youth. Death carousel.

87)
Gourmet serial killer
Hannibal the Cannibal
profiles trans slasher.

88)
Vet's PTSD
Bad trip has him seeing things.
army drugs. Death cheats.

89)
Steals books and boyfriend.
Spellcraft. Shape-shifts. Inherits.
Teen witches' glamour.

90)
Teen sisters' hormones.
Werewolf bite; puberty change.
Murder-spree party.

91)
Snowbound writer crash.
In nurse Annie's care bedfast.
Hobbled typewriter.

Illustration by Emily Broussard

92)
He wakes from coma.
Psychic, sees fire. Politics
gone wrong. Changed future.

93)
Maniac killer,
Scalps girls for mannequins.
Mommy issues.

94)
Her Renfield is 12.
She drinks blood, drowns his bullies.
Blood on Swedish snow.

95)
Blind dead, killer monks,
Revenants shuffle slowly.
Spanish zombie knights.

96)
Couple moves into
Haunted house. Witch Angelique
Seduces artist.

97)
Abby Normal's brain
Helps grandson create
Tap-dancing creature.

Illustration by Emily Broussard

98)
Brothers kidnap fam.
RV. Mexico. Strip club.
Vampire queen with snake.

99)
Jazz musician sees
Psychic killed, window bloody.
Breaks into killer's house.

100)
Black Phillip beckons.
Nude witches join coven dance.
Live deliciously!

INDEX to ILLUSTRATIONS

It's only a spoiler if you know the name of the movie.

SPOILER INDEX of MOVIE TITLES

1   Jaws (1975)

2   Psycho (1960)

3   Halloween (1978)

4   Demons (1985)

5   Peeping Tom (1960)

6   Black Sunday (1960)

7   Jack Frost (1997)

8   Creature From the Black Lagoon (1954) /
    Shape Of Water (2017)

9   Creature from the Black Lagoon (1954)

10 Trick 'R Treat (2007)

11 House On Haunted Hill (1959)

12 Friday The 13th Part 1 (1980)

13 Friday The 13th Part 3 (1982)

14 Deathgasm (2015)

15 Nightmare On Elm Street Part 2 (1985)

16 Sleepaway Camp (1983)

17 The Hills Have Eyes (1977)

18 Lair of the White Worm (1988)

19 American Werewolf in London (1981)

20 The Wolfman (1941/2010)

-100 HAIKUS about HORROR MOVIES-

SPOILER INDEX of MOVIE TITLES

SPOILER INDEX of MOVIE TITLES

SPOILER INDEX of MOVIE TITLES

SPOILER INDEX of MOVIE TITLES

ABOUT THE AUTHOR

S.L. Skinner is a horror film enthusiast and poet. Interests include cryptid taxidermy, palmistry, bibliomancy, canning pickled punks, kung fu movies, and fine art appreciation.

When not sewing the good part of a unicorn to the bad part of a gryphon, the author enjoys: horror anime, indie anthologies, old copies of Fangoria with questionably sticky pages, playing exquisite corpse, and all things Tom Savini.

 Skinner cultivates a chupacabra sanctuary near Marfa, Texas off Pinto Canyon Road. The author practices shibari goat roping in their spare time as a form of active meditation, and as a way to nurture the cryptids in the nature preserve. Next door you can visit the Cabrito BBQ joint and taste their tangy, secret sauce.

All haikus were composed under full moonlight in the author's writing nook nestled in a cave in the rugged canyons of the Chinati Mountains. On dark nights, you can see the flickering projection of old Roger Corman movies against the cliff face. If you tune in your car stereo just right, you might get sound.

With a mug of hot witches' brew and a smoldering desire to review 100 horror movies, Skinner's poetic take on scary cinema ranges from silent film serial killers to post-modern murder-fests, and features frightening films in dialects from around the globe that speak the universal human language of fear, revulsion, and horror.

Made in the USA
Las Vegas, NV
21 October 2024

10257326R00029